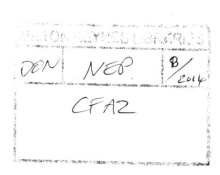

A catalogue record for this book is available
from the British Library

Published by Ladybird Books Ltd
A subsidiary of the Penguin Group
A Pearson Company

Text copyright © FREDERICK WARNE & CO., MCMXCII
Illustrations from *The World of Peter Rabbit and Friends*™
animated television series made for Frederick Warne and
T.V. Cartoons Ltd by Grand Slamm Partnership
Copyright © FREDERICK WARNE & CO., MCMXCII/VI
© In presentation LADYBIRD BOOKS LTD MCMXCII/VI

LADYBIRD and the device of a Ladybird are trademarks of
Ladybird Books Ltd Loughborough Leicestershire UK

THE
TALE OF
BENJAMIN
BUNNY ™

Based on the original and authorized story
by Beatrix Potter
Ladybird Books in association with Frederick Warne

One morning, young Benjamin
Bunny sat on a bank, watching
the world go by.

Trit-trot, trit-trot! A pony and gig
went past. The gig was driven by
Mr McGregor and beside him sat
Mrs McGregor, wearing her best
bonnet.

As soon as they had passed, little
Benjamin Bunny set off with a hop,
skip and a jump to visit his Aunt and
cousins, who lived in a wood at the
back of Mr McGregor's garden.

In the woods, Benjamin almost
tumbled over his cousin Peter, who
was sitting by himself wrapped
in a red cotton handkerchief.
He looked poorly.

"What's the matter?" asked Benjamin.

"I went into Mr McGregor's garden yesterday," sniffed Peter. "He chased me away. When I got home Mama gave me some camomile tea and put me to bed."

Benjamin looked at the red cotton handkerchief.

"Where are your clothes?" he asked.

"I lost them in Mr McGregor's garden," said Peter. "Now the scarecrow is wearing them."

"Let's get them back," said Benjamin.
"Mr and Mrs McGregor have gone out
for the day. Mrs McGregor was
wearing her best bonnet."

"I hope it rains," said Peter Rabbit.

Hand in hand, the little rabbits made
their way to Mr McGregor's garden.
They jumped up onto his wall and
looked down.

There was the scarecrow.

It was dressed with Peter's coat and shoes, topped with an old tam-o-shanter belonging to Mr McGregor.

Benjamin climbed down a pear tree and reached the garden safely. Peter fell down head first, but he did not hurt himself because of the soft, newly raked soil.

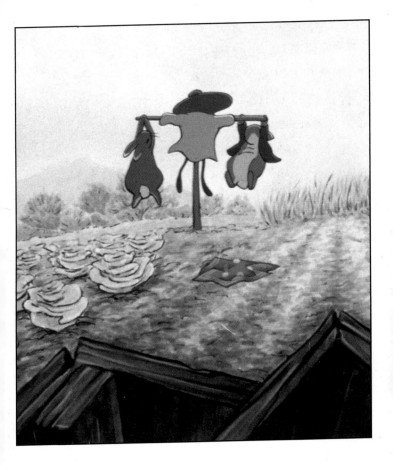

The two little rabbits ran over to the
scarecrow. Unfortunately, they left
little foot-marks all over the garden
beds, especially Benjamin, who was
wearing clogs.

Benjamin and Peter rescued Peter Rabbit's clothes. There had been rain during the night; the coat was somewhat shrunk and there was water in the shoes. Benjamin Bunny tried on the tam-o-shanter, but it was too big for him.

Then Benjamin suggested that they fill the red cotton handkerchief with onions as a present for his Aunt.

But Peter wanted to go home. He kept hearing noises. Benjamin, on the contrary, was perfectly at home and ate a lettuce leaf.

Little Benjamin said that
they couldn't climb the pear tree
carrying a load of vegetables. He led
the way boldly to the other end of the
garden. As they walked along, Peter
dropped the onions.

They landed amongst some flower-pots, and frames and tubs.
Peter and Benjamin scrambled to pick them up and this is what they saw round the corner!

Quick as a flash, Benjamin hid
himself and Peter and the onions
underneath a large basket.

The cat got up and stretched herself.
Then she came over to sniff at the
basket. Perhaps she liked the smell of
onions, because she sat down on top
of the basket.

She stayed there for *five* hours!

It was dark inside the basket and the smell of onions was terrible. Soon, Peter Rabbit and little Benjamin began to cry.

At length there was a pitter-patter, pitter-patter. The cat looked up and saw old Mr Bouncer walking along the terrace wall. He was smoking a pipe of rabbit-tobacco and had a little switch in his hand. He was looking for his son.

Mr Bouncer had no opinion whatever of cats. He jumped off the wall and landed on the cat. Then he cuffed it and kicked it into the green-house.

Mr Bouncer locked the green-house
door and came back to the basket. He
took Benjamin out by the ears, giving
him a smack with the switch, and
pulled out his nephew Peter.

Then Mr Bouncer picked up the handkerchief of onions, pulled up a fine young lettuce by the root and marched out of the garden.

When Mr McGregor returned, he was puzzled to see that somebody had been walking all over his garden in a pair of clogs – and the footprints were very, very small!

Also, he could not understand how
the cat had managed to shut herself
up *inside* the green-house, locking the
door from the *outside*.

When Peter got home, his mother
forgave him for being late because
she was glad to see that he had found
his shoes and coat.

And, whilst Peter and his sister Cotton-tail folded up the red cotton handkerchief, Mrs Rabbit strung up the onions and hung them from the kitchen ceiling.